MINNESOTA
TWINS

AL WEST

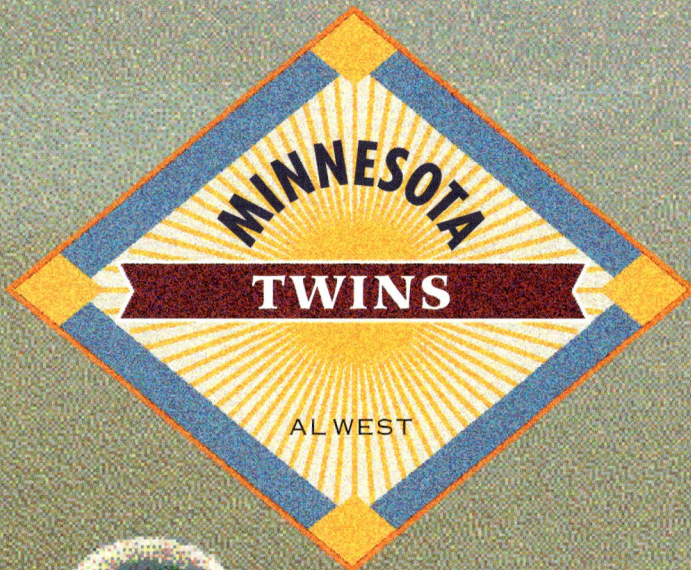

RICHARD RAMBECK

Published by Creative Education, Inc.

123 S. Broad Street, Mankato, Minnesota 56001

Art Director, Rita Marshall
Cover and title page design by Virginia Evans
Cover and title page illustration by Rob Day
Type set by FinalCopy Electronic Publishing
Book design by Rita Marshall

Photos by Focus on Sports, National Baseball Library,
Spectra-Action, Sportschrome West, Sports Illustrated,
UPI/Bettmann, Ron Vesley and Wide World Photos

Library of Congress Cataloging-in-Publication Data

Rambeck, Richard.

    Minnesota Twins / by Richard Rambeck.

    p. cm.

    Summary: A team history of the Minnesota Twins,
a franchise begun as the Washington Senators, but
resident of the Twin Cities area since 1961.

    ISBN 0-88682-446-X

    1. Minnesota Twins (Baseball team)—History—
Juvenile literature.   [1. Minnesota Twins (Baseball
team)—History. 2. Baseball—History.] I. Title.
GV875.M55R36 1991   91-10140
796.357'64'09776579—dc20   CIP

THE EARLY YEARS

Minnesota's Twin Cities—Minneapolis and St. Paul—are the two largest towns in the place known as both the North Star State and the Gopher State. In fact, the metropolitan area that includes the Twin Cities accounts for more than half the 4.3 million people who live in Minnesota. The Twin Cities are located on the eastern edge of the state, on the Mississippi River and near the Minnesota-Wisconsin border. The Mississippi actually divides the two cities: Minneapolis is on the west side of the river, and St. Paul is on the east.

The Twin Cities are the center of economic and government activity in Minnesota. There are several major barge lines operating out of Minneapolis and St. Paul that carry goods down the mighty Mississippi to other fresh-

Hall of Famer Harmon Killebrew.

Camilo Pascual led the Twins' pitching staff in victories, ERA and strikeouts.

water ports. In addition, St. Paul is the capital of Minnesota, so it is home to the governor and the state legislature.

The Twin Cities area is also home to a rich sports tradition that includes the Minnesota Vikings of the National Football League, the Minnesota North Stars of the National Hockey League, the Minnesota Timberwolves of the National Basketball Association, and the Minnesota Twins, who since 1961 have been members of the American League of professional baseball. The Minnesota baseball franchise actually began in Washington, D.C., and was known as the Senators. But Washington owner Calvin Griffith was unhappy with the fan support in the nation's capital, so he moved the team to the Twin Cities area in 1961 and changed the nickname to the Twins.

Griffith's club may not have had many fans in Washington, but Minnesota residents took to the team right away. More than twenty four thousand showed up for opening day in 1961, and the Twins drew nearly 1.5 million fans their first year. The club played its home games in Metropolitan Stadium, which actually wasn't located in either Minneapolis or St. Paul, but was in Bloomington, a city that is considered part of the Twin Cities metropolitan area.

HARMON HAMMERS HOMERS

Although Minnesota wasn't a championship-caliber ball club at first, the team did bring several budding stars with it from Washington. The best of these was a stocky, muscular slugger named Harmon Killebrew.

A great pitcher in any city, Frank Viola.

Harmon Killebrew set a Minnesota record by belting 49 home runs during the season.

Killebrew began his major-league career in 1954, when he was just seventeen years old. He soon established himself as one of the finest home-run hitters in baseball. Killebrew led the American League in homers five times during his years with the Twins, including three straight seasons, from 1962 through 1964.

Hammerin' had a no-nonsense approach to hitting. While waiting in the on-deck circle, he would stand virtually motionless and glare at the pitcher. Then he would take three or four ferocious swings before kneeling and resuming his glare. Once in the batter's box, the right-handed hitter would allow himself one calming swish of the bat between pitches. Otherwise, he stood absolutely still, with the bat just resting on his shoulder.

"I'm not a fidgety person," Killebrew explained. "I try to stay as calm and relaxed as I can. It helps me concentrate, which I think is the most important thing about hitting." As his career progressed, he started to hit for a much higher average, something he attributed to the knowledge that comes as a veteran. "Naturally, I hope I've gotten smarter as I've gotten more experience," he said. "But I can't get all that excited about the .300 thing. The important thing for me is to drive in runs and score them. I think I should take the hardest swings I can every time I'm at the plate." Killebrew's trademark remained the long ball throughout his brilliant career. He wound up hitting 573 home runs, making him fifth on the list of all-time home run hitters. He slammed a homer an average of once every 12.9 times at bat—just a notch behind Babe Ruth's record of one homer every 11.8 times up.

Killebrew wasn't the Twins' only outstanding hitter, however. Rookie Tony Oliva made a tremendous first-year impression by winning the American League batting title in 1964. (Oliva also repeated that feat in 1965.) For his efforts, Oliva was named the American League Rookie of the Year in 1964. Both Killebrew and Oliva had outstanding years in 1965, but shortstop Zoilo Versalles had the season of a lifetime. The speedster led the American League in runs scored and was second in hits, first in doubles, second in triples, and third in stolen bases. To no one's surprise, Versalles was named the American League's Most Valuable Player.

Led by Versalles, the Twins posted a 102–60 record in 1965, which is still a franchise record for victories in a season, and won the American League pennant. It was the first time in six years that a team other than the New York Yankees had won the American league title. The Twins had aced out one team with a rich tradition for the pennant and faced another proud team in the World Series—the Los Angeles Dodgers. If the Twins were in awe of the powerful Dodgers, they didn't show it. Minnesota won the first two games of the series, both played in Metropolitan Stadium, defeating Los Angeles pitching aces Don Drysdale and Sandy Koufax in the process. Los Angeles then won all three games at home and returned to Minnesota with a 3–2 lead in the series. The Twins rebounded for a 5–1 victory in game six, but then Koufax tossed a shutout in the seventh game as the Dodgers won it all with a 2–0 victory.

1 9 6 5

Twins' shortstop Zoilo Versalles was named the AL MVP for leading the club to their first pennant.

CAREW HITS, AND HITS, AND HITS

The young Twins had been beaten, but they were determined to get back to the World Series. It

10   *Another great Twins' hitter, Brian Harper.*

All-time great, Tony Oliva.

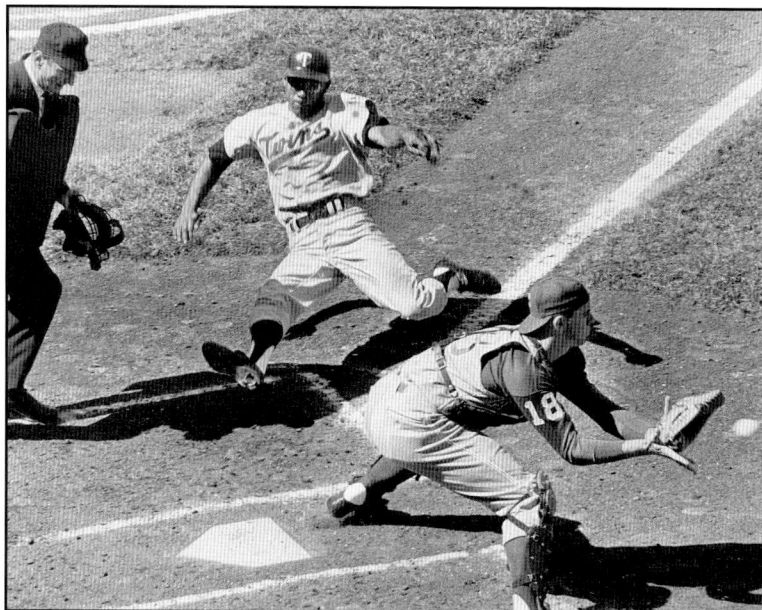

Zoilo Versalles (right) completed his seventh and final season in a Twins' uniform.

seemed as if they would have plenty of chances, with such hitting stars as Killebrew, Versalles, and Oliva. The pitching staff was ably manned by Jim "Mudcat" Grant, Jim Perry, Dean Chance, and Jim Kaat. As if that weren't enough talent, the Twins found another star in 1967, a sweet-swinging second baseman named Rod Carew.

Carew showed his awesome potential immediately as he was named the American League Rookie of the Year in 1967. Two years later he won the first of seven batting titles as a Minnesota player. The left-handed hitter was born in Panama and grew up as a typical Latin American player, a free-swinger. "My own theory," Carew stated when asked if he waited for the right pitch, "is swing the bat. If the ball's around the plate, swing and make contact. I grew up that way in Panama. Here [in the United States], a lot of guys look for certain pitches, in certain areas. But you may never get those pitches."

Carew's free-swinging approach and superb bat control baffled opposing fielders. "There's no way you can play him because he can hit with enough power to keep you back deep, so you can't play him like he's going to drop everything over the infield," Oakland A's outfielder Bill North asserted. "And he can drop it over the infield. Rod Carew is in a class all by himself."

Carew often said his favorite kind of hit was one "just one inch or two outside a guy's reach. Maybe he cheated over a step in the other direction on me, and I kept him honest. I hit the ball to the opposite field so much that sometimes they'll move everybody to the left side against me. But I just take my natural swing."

Carew may have won the batting title in 1969, but it was Harmon Killebrew who got most of the headlines for Minnesota. The thirty-two-year-old slugger topped the league in homers with forty-nine, a total that has not been exceeded by any American League player since. Killebrew also led the league in runs batted in with 140. He was named the American League's Most Valuable Player, and his heroics sparked the Twins to the AL West Division title. (The league was split into two divisions in 1969 after the addition of two expansion franchises.) Minnesota advanced to play in the American League Championship Series against East Division winner Baltimore. The powerful Orioles had registered 109 victories during the regular season, twelve more than the Twins. Minnesota wasn't expected to give the Orioles much trouble, and the Twins didn't, losing the best-of-five series with three straight defeats.

In his first and last year as manager, Billy Martin led the Twins to the AL West title.

1 9 7 2

Rod Carew led the Twins in hitting for the first of seven consecutive seasons.

Minnesota actually came back stronger in 1970, taking the AL West again with a 98–64 record, but the team once again ran headlong into the Baltimore Orioles in the league championship series. Baltimore dispatched the Twins and went on to claim the World Series title by beating National League champion Cincinnati. Minnesota's string of successes had come to an end. The team had won the first two American League West Division championships, but the franchise would have to wait seventeen years for its next title. Twins stars such as Killebrew, Oliva, and Jim Perry were getting old. As a result, Minnesota soon fell behind rising powers Oakland and Kansas City in the AL West. The Twins staggered to a 74–86 record in 1971, despite Tony Oliva's remarkable year. He won his third American League batting title by hitting .337, a career high.

The following year, Rod Carew succeeded Oliva as American League batting champ, a title he would win four consecutive years. Carew and Dutch-born pitcher Bert Blyleven provided many of the highlights for the Twins, whose glory years slipped further and further behind them. In the late 1970s, Minnesota owner Calvin Griffith became known as someone who would sell most of his high-paid veterans and replace them with younger players who had very low salaries. Griffith also made no effort to try to acquire quality players as free agents. As a result, attendance at aging Metropolitan Stadium dropped as fast as the team's fortunes.

As the 1980s approached, the Twins were going nowhere. Rod Carew, who was voted American League MVP in 1977, was finally traded to the California Angels for young outfielder Ken Landreaux and several other

Like Carew before him, Kirby Puckett is an AL batting champ.

untried players. The Twins celebrated their twentieth year in 1981, but the team wound up in last place. Then, just as it started to look as if Minnesota's fortunes would never improve, the team's luck started to change. A big reason for the change was a power-hitting first baseman who had grown up in the Twin Cities area.

HRBEK BECOMES FIRST STAR AMONG "NEW" TWINS

Kent Hrbek was born in Minneapolis on May 21, 1960. Twenty-one years later, Hrbek was on the verge of joining his hometown major-league team. The power-hitting first baseman was playing for Visalia of the California League in 1981. The Twins, who had traded away star first baseman Rod Carew, were ready to give the six-foot-four, 220-pound Hrbek a shot at the big time.

The often-injured John Castino.

Slugger Kent Hrbek

A year later (1982) Hrbek was joined by another minor league star, slugger Tom Brunansky.

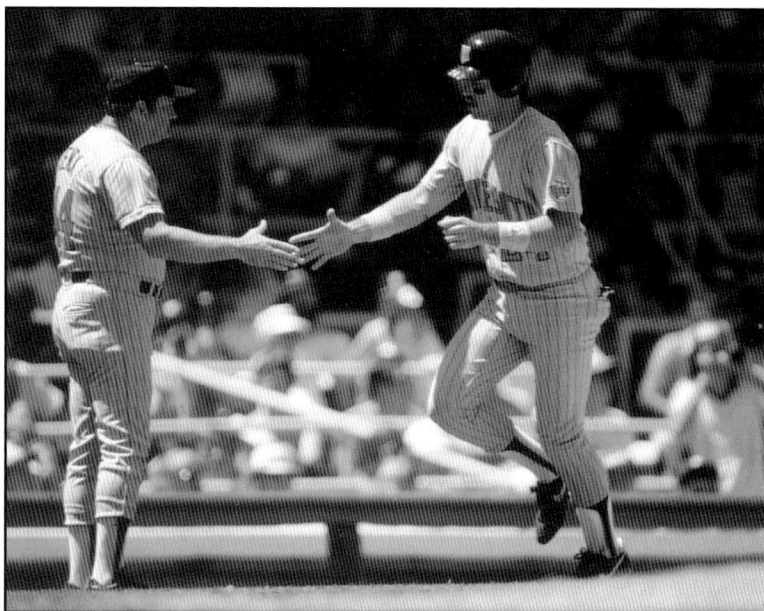

"The last week before I was called up [to the majors], this clothing store [in Visalia] had a promotion in which it would give away a pair of pants to the first player who hit a home run in a game," Hrbek laughed. "I think I won four pairs that week. I had to order them by phone, though, because I was already in the major leagues."

Hrbek may have been in the big leagues, but he had a hard time believing it. His first game as a Minnesota Twin was in New York's historic Yankee Stadium, and Hrbek was clearly star-struck. "I watched Reggie Jackson and Dave Winfield run by, and I wanted to just go up and meet them and shake their hands," Hrbek recalled. "If I'd had a pen and paper, I'd have asked for their autographs."

Hrbek was installed as the Twins designated hitter in the series against the Yankees. In the first game, Hrbek came up to hit in the twelfth inning with the score tied. He proceeded to hit a home run that eventually won the game. "What I had done really didn't hit me until I got home a few days later," Hrbek said of his Yankee Stadium blast. "I woke up one morning, and there on the wall was a picture of Yankee Stadium I had put up as a kid."

Minnesota teammates called Hrbek "The Kid," but this "kid" was hitting like a man. His performance at the end of the 1981 season was good enough to earn him a permanent place on the Twins roster for 1982, which was the year the Twins acquired a new home. The franchise moved into the Hubert H. Humphrey Metrodome, a sturdy, weatherproof structure that featured a ten-acre roof made of Teflon-coated fiberglass. The team's home park was new, but the results were the same as before. Minnesota finished the season with a 60–102 record, worst among the twenty-six major-league teams.

Hrbek was one of the few Twins capable of terrorizing opposing pitchers. However, help was soon on the way. While Hrbek was making his impression on American League pitching, the Twins selected a stocky outfielder named Kirby Puckett in the first round of the 1982 amateur draft. It would prove to be one of the best choices the team ever made.

Puckett's first full year in the majors, 1984, was a big one not only for him, but also for the Minnesota franchise. Calvin Griffith, who had owned the team even before it moved from Washington, D.C., to Minnesota, finally agreed to sell the Twins. Many predicted Griffith would sell to one of several ownership groups that wanted to buy the team and move it to another city. But

In his first full season with the Twins, Kent Hrbek was named to the AL West All-Star team.

Gold Glove winner Gary Gaetti.

Minnesota businessman Carl Pohlad stepped forward and offered to buy the franchise for $35 million. Pohlad's decision assured that the club would stay in the Twin Cities.

The team responded to the ownership change positively, and so did the fans. Almost 1.6 million people attended Twins home games during the 1984 season, marking the first time since 1979 that the club had drawn more than one million. In addition, the Twins were in a pennant race for the first time in several years. Minnesota wound up with an 81–81 record, which was only three games behind American League West Division champion Kansas City. The Twins remained about a .500 team in 1985 and 1986, mainly because the team's pitching wasn't good enough to support the excellent hitting of Puckett, Hrbek, third baseman Gary Gaetti, and outfielder Tom Brunansky. But that would change in 1987.

There was a different attitude in the Twins training camp in 1987. In large part, it was due to manager Tom Kelly, who, at age thirty-six, was the youngest skipper in the majors. "I like to keep the game fun," the low-key Kelly explained. One of the reasons Kelly expected the game to be fun for the Twins was the acquisition of ace relief pitcher Jeff Reardon from the Montreal Expos. "Remember," Kelly recalled before the season started, "this club lost twenty-seven games last year [1986] from the seventh inning on. If Reardon can close the door for us this year, we think the rest of our lineup can have a lot more fun, too."

Kelly proved to be a prophet. Reardon notched thirty-one saves, and he complemented an improved staff of starting pitchers that included lefty Frank Viola (17–10,

1 9 8 6

Bert Blyleven equalled his 1974 performance by leading the team in wins, ERA and strikeouts.

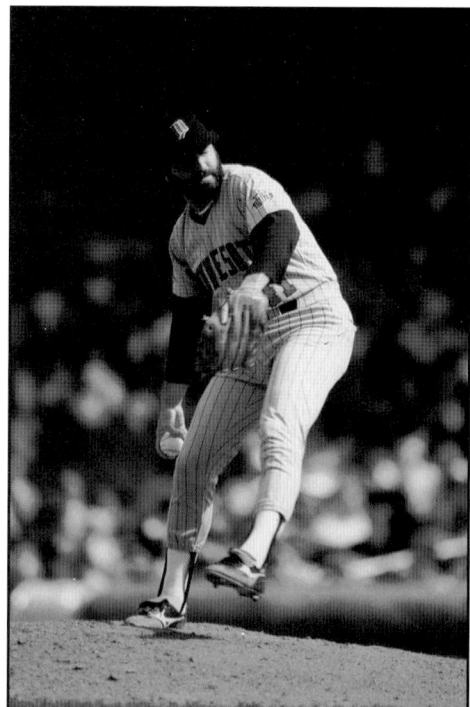

24   *Left to right: Bert Blyleven, Roy Smalley, Dan Gladden, Jeff Reardon.*

2.90 earned-run average) and right-hander Bert Blyleven (15–12). The Twins also got great years from Puckett (.332 average, twenty-eight homers, ninety-nine RBI), Hrbek (.285 average, thirty-four homers, ninety RBI), Gaetti (thirty-one homers, 109 RBI), and Brunansky (thirty-two homers, eighty-five RBI).

Minnesota wound up winning its first AL West Division title in seventeen years, posting an 85–77 record. In the American League Championship Series, the Twins weren't expected to do well against the Detroit Tigers, who had won ninety-eight games. But Minnesota captured the first two games, in the Metrodome, and the Tigers never recovered. After beating Detroit four games to one, the Twins advanced to their first World Series in twenty-two years. Again, no one expected Minnesota to beat the powerful St. Louis Cardinals, who had the best record in the National League. But the Twins had two things going for them: the Metrodome and Frank Viola.

During the 1987 World Series, history was made. For the first time, World Series games were played indoors. And the Metrodome wasn't just any dome; it was such a noisy place, opposing teams absolutely hated to play there. The Cardinals undoubtedly felt that way after losing 10–1 and 8–4 in the first two games of the series. Luckily for the Cards, the series then shifted outdoors to Busch Stadium in St. Louis, where the home team won games three, four, and five to take a 3–2 lead. Back in the Metrodome, the Cardinals streaked to a 5–2 lead in game six and were on the verge of closing out the series, but designated hitter Don Baylor slammed a two-run homer and Kent Hrbek supplied the biggest blow of the series, a grand-slam home run in the sixth inning that

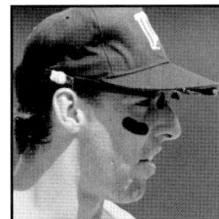

1 9 8 7

Gary Gaetti became the first player in history to homer in his first two post-season at-bats.

gave the Twins a 10–5 lead. Minnesota wound up winning 11–5.

Manager Tom Kelly then gave Viola—winner in game one, loser in game four—the starting call in game seven. The Twins ace gave up two runs in the second inning, but that was all he would surrender. Minnesota scored single runs in the second, fifth, sixth, and eighth innings to claim a 4–2 victory and the first World Series title in Minnesota history. Viola was named series MVP, and the Metrodome, where the Twins won all four games, was clearly MVS—Most Valuable Stadium.

The Twins had reached the top very quickly after struggling for years near the bottom of the AL West. But they have not yet managed to build on their 1987 World Series triumph. Minnesota, in fact, fell to fifth place in the division in 1988. The decline forced management to think about making changes. Brunansky and Viola were both traded, as was Bert Blyleven.

1 9 8 9

After winning 17 games, Allan Anderson became the AL's winningest pitcher over the past two seasons.

TWINS GO BOWLING WITH PUCKETT

While the Twins' fortunes declined, the play of Kirby Puckett just got better and better. In 1989 he became the first Twin since Rod Carew to win a batting title. Puckett confounded the so-called experts, who wondered how he could be so good with such an odd physique. He resembles a bowling ball more than a baseball player. Puckett is listed at five-foot-eight and carries at least 210 pounds on his stocky frame. "You look at him, and you think he's a fat little kid," recalled former Minnesota manager Ray Miller. "You touch him, and he's like concrete."

A man for all positions. The multi-talented Al Newman takes a throw from home.

Puckett, who always seems to be smiling, is also a positive influence on the other Twins, and his shaved head has become the team's rabbit's foot. "The guys rub my head and relax," Puckett explained. "I don't care what people think. Somebody's got to be the good-luck charm." Puckett may be a symbol of luck for his teammates, but he is the one who feels lucky. "I love the game. This is fun for me. It was fun when I was a kid. It is now. I didn't play baseball so I could get out of the ghetto. I played baseball because I enjoyed baseball. And now look, I'm in the big leagues." Twins second baseman Al Newman admitted he was amazed by Puckett's attitude and ability. "He's got this charisma," Newman asserted. "He's always smiling. I've never heard him booed. When I first came here, I said, 'How can this guy throw? How can he hit?' He's the eighth wonder of the world."

Lefty Allan Anderson.

Young star Scott Erickson.

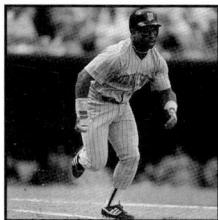

Despite the loss of Gary Gaetti, the Twins and Kirby Puckett were much improved.

The biggest cause of wonder about Puckett initially was his ability to hit for a high average, which is quite unusual for a free-swinger who doesn't draw many walks. "He's not going to slump often because he makes contact, runs well, bunts, and knows how to hit in here [the Metrodome]," said Minnesota minor-league director Jim Rantz. Puckett, though, wasn't sure he was doing much of anything right at the plate. "When I learn to discipline myself," he explained, "I'll be a better hitter."

The Twins hope that, with Puckett leading the way, they will become a better team. Minnesota needs to get solid performances from Kent Hrbek and Gary Gaetti, both of whom are trying to rebound from some sub-par years. The Twins also are counting on quality play from outfielders Dan Gladden and Shane Mack, and catcher Brian Harper. The pitching staff—minus Frank Viola and Jeff Reardon—is young but improving. Allan Anderson won seventeen games in 1989 and has shown, that despite an off-year in 1990, he is one of the top left-handers in the American League. Rick Aguilera and Kevin Tapani, both acquired from the New York Mets in the trade for Viola, have shown promise.

If the pitching continues to get better, the Twins should become contenders in the powerful AL West. Thanks to the talents of Puckett, Hrbek, Harper, Gladden, and Gaetti, Minnesota is one of the top hitting teams in the American League. And that element—great hitting—has been a consistent feature of the Twins franchise for the last thirty years.